Outdoor Adventure Parks

Jill McDougall

Contents

What Are Outdoor Adventure Parks?

Outdoor adventure parks are places where people can try exciting outdoor activities.

There are many kinds of adventure parks. Some parks have lots of water sports for people to do, such as riding water slides or paddling canoes.

Some outdoor adventure parks have big water slides.

Other adventure parks have activities like **zip lining** or horse riding.

Many children enjoy adventure parks because they can take **risks** in a safe place.

Zip lining is a fun activity people can try at an outdoor adventure park.

People work in many different jobs at an adventure park.

Some workers, such as lifeguards, help to keep visitors safe. Other people keep the park clean, or sell food and drinks.

Lifeguards make sure everyone is safe in the water at adventure parks.

Most outdoor adventure parks have activities for everyone in the family to enjoy.

People often buy a ticket for a whole day.

After buying their tickets, people enter the adventure park and begin a day of activities.

Giant Mazes

Some outdoor adventure parks have giant mazes
that can be lots of fun for everyone.

People start at one end of the maze
and walk along the paths
until they find their way out.

It is easy to get lost in a giant maze!
There are lots of **dead ends**,
so people have to turn around
and try going a different way.

The sides of a maze can be made from wood, **hedges** or even hay.

Sometimes, there is a tower in the middle of a maze. If someone is lost, they can climb up the tower to look for the way out.

This giant maze is made up of lots of big hay **bales**.

Some mazes are enormous!
One of the biggest mazes in the world is in China.
To make this huge maze,
people planted 1000 trees.
Later, the little trees were cut into long hedges.

This is a bird's-eye view of the huge maze in China.
Part of it is in the shape of a giant deer.

Water Parks

Water parks are like big, watery outdoor playgrounds. They have activities for people of all ages.

Young children can play in shallow pools that have water sprays and little slides.

Some pools have tipping buckets that dump water with a big *splash*.

Little children splash around in shallow pools at water parks.

Water parks sometimes have wave pools, too. The waves are made by a machine.

When the waves are very high, it can be thrilling and scary!

Being in a wave pool can feel like you are in the ocean!

Another exciting activity at water parks is zooming down a water slide.

These slides have water flowing down them to make the slide slippery.

Water slides usually have lots of twists and turns. Sometimes, they have dark tunnels to ride through!

On some water slides, more than one rider can go down at once.

Racing water slides have lanes side by side, so people can race one another to the pool below.

Other water slides are wide enough for people to ride down together on a raft.

Mini Golf

Some outdoor adventure parks have places to play mini golf.

There are 18 holes on a mini-golf course. Players go from hole to hole, hitting their golf ball into each one. They use a special golf club called a putter.

The winner is the player who gets their ball into all 18 holes in the least number of hits.

People of all ages can have fun on a mini-golf course.

Playing mini golf can be harder than it looks. On a mini-golf course, there can be rocks and logs or even small sandpits.

Sometimes, players have to hit their ball through a little tunnel or across a narrow bridge.

All of these things make it harder for players to hit their ball into the hole!

Mini golf is also called putt-putt.

Sometimes people need to hit their ball around rocks to reach the hole in mini golf.

High Ropes Courses

In some outdoor adventure parks, people do activities way up high in the treetops.
These are called high ropes courses.

To start the ropes course, people must first climb up to a **platform**.
The platform is built around the trunk of a tree.

People move across to other platforms by walking along bridges made of rope.

People begin a high ropes course from a wooden platform around a tree.

High ropes courses are exciting, but people must follow the safety rules.

The climbers wear a **harness** that is tied to a strong rope. The harness stops people from falling to the ground if they lose their balance.

Climbers wear a safety helmet, too.

It is important to wear a helmet and a harness for safety when on a high ropes course.

Some high ropes courses end with a fun ride on a zip line. People clip their harness onto a line that carries them quickly back to the ground.

High ropes courses can be enjoyed by people of all different ages. There are easy courses for young children and harder ones for older people.

Riding a zip line can feel like flying through the air!

A visit to an outdoor adventure park can be full of exciting new discoveries.

Outdoor adventure parks are great places to have fun with family and friends.

Glossary

bales (*noun*)	large bunches of hay that have been tied together
dead ends (*noun*)	endings to roads or pathways with no way to keep going
harness (*noun*)	a set of straps used to attach a person or animal to something
hedges (*noun*)	rows of bushes grown close together and then cut evenly to make a barrier
platform (*noun*)	a raised floor or surface
risks (*noun*)	actions that might cause danger to a person
zip lining (*noun*)	when a person rides quickly along a rope stretched between two trees while they are attached to a harness

Index